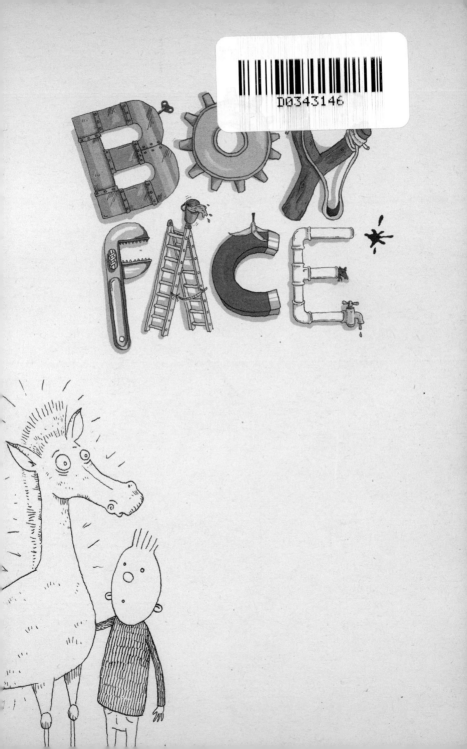

Have you read the other
Boyface books? ...

BOYFACE AND THE QUANTUM CHROMATIC DISRUPTION MACHINE

BOYFACE AND THE TARTAN BADGER

BOYFACE AND THE POWER OF THREE AND A BIT

BOY FACE

AND THE UNCERTAIN PONIES

WRITTEN BY
JAMES CAMPBELL

ILLUSTRATED BY
MARK WEIGHTON

Hodder Children's Books

A division of Hachette Children's Books

For the Donaghy family: Juliet, David, Michael, Heather and Steve. With love, J.C.

For Noah H – here's to the out breath. With love M.W.

Text copyright © 2015 James Campbell
Illustrations copyright © 2015 Mark Weighton

First published in Great Britain in 2015
by Hodder Children's Books

The rights of James Campbell and Mark Weighton to be identified as
the Author and Illustrator respectively of the Work have been asserted by
them in accordance with the Copyright, Designs and Patents Act 1988.

All rights reserved. Apart from any use permitted under UK
copyright law, this publication may only be reproduced, stored or
transmitted, in any form, or by any means with prior permission in
writing from the publishers or in the case of reprographic production in
accordance with the terms of licences issued by the Copyright Licensing
Agency and may not be otherwise circulated in any form of binding
or cover other than that in which it is published and without a similar
condition being imposed on the subsequent purchaser.

All characters in this publication are fictitious and any resemblance
to real persons, living or dead, is purely coincidental.

A Catalogue record for this book is available from the British Library.

ISBN: 978 1 444 91805 2

Printed and bound in Great Britain by
CPI Group (UK) Ltd, Croydon, CR0 4YY

The paper and board used in this paperback by Hodder Children's Books
are natural recyclable products made from wood grown in sustainable
forests. The manufacturing processes conform to the environmental
regulations of the country of origin.

Hodder Children's Books
A division of Hachette Children's Books
338 Euston Road, London NW1 3BH
An Hachette UK company
www.hachette.co.uk

Contents:

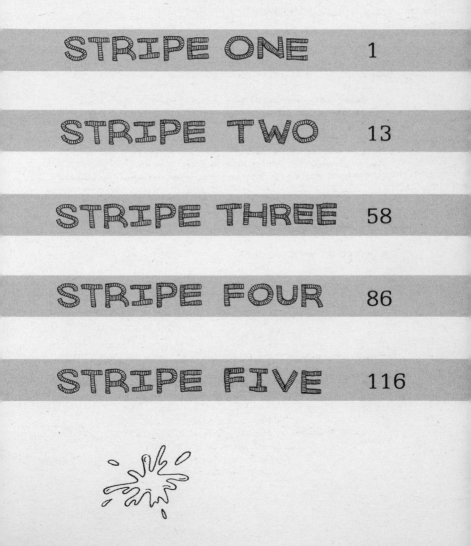

STRIPE ONE

SOME time ago — not that much time, but slightly more than this. No, not like that. Well, imagine if half an afternoon could be multiplied by a long weekend, minus a day off school because you're reasonably poorly. That amount of time. Yes, that's it. Just right. Anyway, about that time ago, there was a village called Stoddenage-on-Sea.

1

The village of Stoddenage-on-Sea looked a bit like someone (probably a giant) had taken a huge bite out of the coastline, chewed it up a bit and then snorted it out, through massive nostrils, in the form of houses and shops, pavements and benches, a small pier, a café and lots and lots of chips. The village was nestled in a pebblish cove between sandy cliffs that towered over the waves like wavy towers.

Usually, people were quite happy in Stoddenage-on-Sea, except when they banged their toes or someone called Adrian kept getting in their way when they were trying to get somewhere in a hurry. The Uncertain Ponies, however, made a lot of people very unhappy indeed.

What is an Uncertain Pony? You may ask. Well, it is a pony that has gone Uncertain.

Ponies rarely look particularly certain of anything, but when they go Uncertain, weird things start to happen. The first pony to go Uncertain looked very uncertain indeed. It was called Tinkerbell and it was being ridden by a slightly podgy little girl called Flotilla.

Flotilla was trotting Tinkerbell around the riding school one day, when the pony started to feel very unusual beneath her. First of all Tinkerbell started wobbling and then started to feel a bit gooey. The little girl didn't have a lot of experience of riding and so she wasn't really sure what was going on. To be honest, even if she had had years of experience of riding, none of those years would have helped her in this situation.

'What's the matter, Tinkerbell?' the child asked. Before the pony had a chance to answer, there was a flash of light, an almighty screech, a bang like the sound of a crash, and a horrible smell like old people's slippers.

Flotilla felt very peculiar for quite a few moments, then looked down to see that her beloved pony was now white with black stripes. It had turned into a zebra. She looked around the field at the other children in the riding school and noticed

that something very strange was
happening to some of the other ponies
as well. Two had turned into zebras
and one looked like it was about to.
The rest looked extremely Uncertain
about who they
were, and where
all the zebras
had come from.

Stoddenage-on-Sea is a small place and as most small places, word travelled fast. It didn't take long before everyone was talking about ponies popping into zebras and pretty soon the whole county was gossiping about what on Earth was going on. Even people who spent most of their time in their sheds, playing with pieces of weird metal, and with no interest in ponies or zebras were talking about it.

Most people would find it quite odd for a pony to turn into a zebra. In fact,

it is quite odd for a pony to suddenly turn into a zebra. It is quite odd for a pony to suddenly turn into anything, apart from maybe a side road, a field, or a beef burger.

One family, however, were not as surprised as most would be. This family was the Antelope family: Mr and Mrs Antelope and their son Boyface. The Antelope family were not actual antelopes, Antelope was just their name. And they were not that surprised at ponies spontaneously turningintozebrasbecausepartoftheir

Stripemongering business involved putting zebras through the Quantum Chromatic Disruption Machine in the Shop. This removed their stripes so the Antelopes could sell them on as ponies to local mums with expensive wellies.

The Antelope family lived in a complicated house that looked like it had been bodged together out of other people's, houses by someone who didn't really know what they were doing. This was because the house had been bodged together by Mrs Antelope from bits of other people's houses. And she didn't really know what she was doing.

The house had begun many years ago as nothing more than a field. Mrs Antelope's first acquisition was a wall. Then some more walls, followed by a bit of roof. Over time, she had stolen balconies, chimneys, bits of bedroom, whole living rooms, and once an entire hairdressing salon. Sometimes she had stolen them by night, sometimes in broad daylight, and sometimes during three-legged races.

Many, many people would complain that part of their house had been stolen and badly glued onto the top of the Antelopes' house but Mrs Antelope would always get away with her crimes for three reasons:

 She was lovely.

 No one knew how she was doing it.

 They were afraid that it might make things worse if they complained.

'Mrs Antelope has stolen my gate,' said one lady.

'I wouldn't complain,' replied a neighbour, 'she might take a fence!'

STRIPE TWO

Early one Wednesday morning, Boyface and his dad were having breakfast. Boyface's mum had made a big pile of ugly looking pancakes and then gone off on one of her property-stealing missions, leaving the two Stripemongers to eat without her. Next to the pile of pancakes there was a big pile of letters. Boyface was a boy like most boys but more so and different. It was part of his job to read any letters that arrived at The Shop. Today, they were all complaints from people who had bought ponies from them in the past.

'There's something wrong with the ponies,' said Boyface to his dad. 'They're turning into zebras.'

'They're not turning into zebras,' corrected Mr Antelope. 'They are turning BACK into zebras.'

He was, of course, right. The ponies had started off as zebras. They weren't changing into something new; they were returning to their original state. The problem was that all of the people who had bought ponies from them didn't know that they were really zebras that the Antelopes had tinkered with.

Mr Antelope took a mouthful of pancake from his fork and said, 'Ah forgnfff fizzerd hpnnnnf.'

This is the sound you make if you say 'I thought this would happen,' when your mouth is full of ugly looking pancake.

'Ahnd ttle pprobliegett hourtze,' continued Mr Antelope.

'What do you mean?' asked Boyface.

'If they've started popping into zebras,' explained Mr Antelope with a burp, 'it means they've gone Uncertain — Uncertain on a quantum level. And that means that they could then turn into something completely different. Like a tree, or an umbrella, or a map of somewhere that hasn't been built yet.'

'So the ponies could turn into anything?' gasped Boyface.

'Anything,' underlined his dad.

Boyface looked at another letter.

Dear Mr Antelope,

What the flumming bling has happened to my son's pony? I bought that pony off of you in good faith and now it has turned into a zebra. Clearly you are up to something very dodgy and probably illegal. I have a good mind to phone the police you scandalous pooflip!

Yours,

Diane McEndemol

Since Boyface had begun his training as a Stripemonger, his skills had grown and grown. At the beginning, Mr Antelope had been very strict about what Boyface was allowed to do and what he wasn't allowed to do. This list on the first page of Boyface's notebook looked like this:

 Watching (not touching)

 Listening (not talking)

 Making massive pots of tea that are almost too heavy to lift (not spilling it)

Sitting still (not moving)

After a while, Boyface was given more responsibilities. These included:

 Answering the phone and taking messages

 Opening and reading letters

 Welcoming customers into The Shop

 Remembering things

 Drinking tea

Pretending that Mr Antelope wasn't available

Slowly, Boyface was learning the business of Stripemongery. Customers would come in to get quotes for jobs they wanted doing, travelling salesman would pop by to sell things like animals, patterns, and ideas. Other customers would swing by to pick up things that Boyface and his dad had put through The Machine. Like Mrs Mulk.

'I want you to do something about

my cat,' she said to Boyface one day, plonking the creature onto the counter.

'I'll just get my dad,' said Boyface, a little scared. Mr Antelope had a look at the cat, turned it upside down, examined its fur with a magnifying glass and polished its nose.

'What's wrong with it?' he asked Mrs Mulk.

'It's rubbish,' explained Mrs Mulk. 'Just look at it. It's brown, and brown

is boring and I want it to be better.'

Mr Antelope took some measurements using a ruler and a pack of butter and wrote some things down on a yellow piece of paper. 'Let me see what I can do,' he said to Mrs Mulk. 'Leave the cat with me and come back later.'

Mrs Mulk went off to do some shopping or something while Mr Antelope and Boyface sat around and wondered about all the things they could do to make a cat better. As often happened, the doorbell tinkled and in came a pair of travelling zookeepers called Barry and Simon. Barry and Simon were old friends of Mr Antelope and brought news that they had a giraffe going cheap in the back of their van. Mr Antelope bought it and pretty soon there was a giraffe standing in the middle of The Shop. Its neck was bent downwards so it didn't bang its head on the ceiling and get all dusty.

'What are we going to do with this?' asked Boyface.

'Well,' mused his dad. 'Let's put it through The Machine, take all its hexagons off, and put them in a bucket.'

They spent the rest of the day removing orange hexagons from the giraffe until it was completely beige. When Mrs Mulk came back from her shopping trip, the Stripemongers were able to suggest that they improve her cat by adding hexagons to it.

She thought that this was an excellent idea and a deal was struck.

The next day, Boyface had the pleasure of presenting Mrs Mulk with her improved cat.

'Not only does it now have hexagons, Mrs Mulk,' he explained to her proudly. 'It will also be quite happy eating trees and never need to be fed again!'

Mrs Mulk wasn't expecting that but she thought it sounded great and paid in full.

And so, Boyface's role was growing and growing in the Stripemongering business. The thing that took time to learn was, of course, Stripemongering itself. Running the business was one thing. Working The Machine was quite another.

'The Machine is quite simple, really,' Boyface would explain to anyone who asked. 'It just alters the vibrational frequency of the things you put in it.' No one was really sure what that meant or whether Boyface knew what he was talking about. In fact, Boyface wasn't sure if he knew what he was talking about but his dad definitely did know that

Boyface did know what he was talking about but that he probably just didn't know that yet.

The Machine was an amazing construction that seemed to be electric and steam-powered and bubbly and alive all at the same time. Mr Antelope and Boyface used The Machine to do the following things:

 Join up the dots on Dalmatians to make rude pictures

 Make wallpaper less terrifying

Make wallpaper more
terrifying

 Create flowers that wouldn't
otherwise exist

 Repair hamsters that have
gone wrong

 Make the lacy bits that go
round underwear for old ladies

 Count pebbles and put them
in order

Make small dogs less annoying

 Make big dogs go fuzzy around the edges

 Teach polar bears to ask silly questions

 Make helmets that protect you from monsters

 Make helmets that protect you from the moon

 Make helmets that protect you from learning things that aren't true

Make helmets that protect you from lemons

 Help leopards change their spots for criminal purposes

 Make gerbils wet themselves

 Create compost out of homework

 Shave cats, cover them in glue and roll them in glitter to make a Disco Cat!

Legends and old books suggested that The Machine could do other, even more amazing things if it was operated in the right way by the right person. Theoretically, it could do the following things:

 Force owls to tell better stories

 Make teapots that fill themselves

 Get rid of unwanted seagulls

 Flatten hills that are in the way

Create rainbows in unusual shapes (e.g. raintriangles, rainsquares, rainhexagons and rainparallelograms)

 Change the weather

 Make fireworks that don't scare dogs

 Make cheese and pickle sandwiches

 Create black holes

Suck the universe up its own bottom

 Go sideways in time

 Make maps of how things, thoughts, and people are connected

 Butter crackers without breaking them

Right at that moment, however, it would have been nice if it could have been used to work out what was the flumming bling was going on with the zebras.

'Maybe it's not our fault,' suggested Boyface. 'Maybe there's something wrong with the zebras. Maybe they were dodgy before we got them.'

This sounded like a possibility to Mr Antelope. He was always very vague when it came to talking about the zebras. He had told Boyface that they came from some country called Bahoumanoomaland. This sounded like a made-up place to Boyface but his dad swore that it was real.

To make things more mysterious, Boyface never saw who sold the zebras to them. The animals arrived once every month when the moon was at its fullest and roundest. The next morning, there would be a pile of wooden crates on the pier with labels on them saying things like:

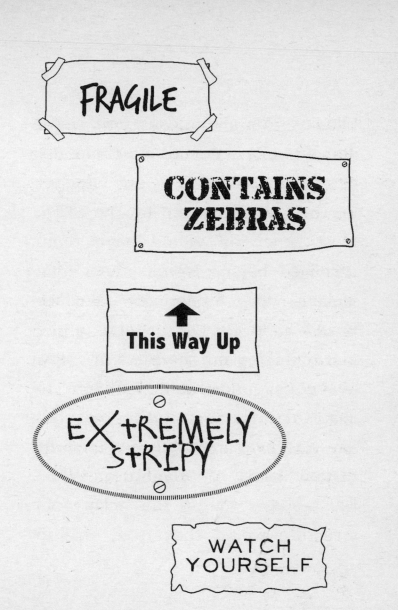

Usually, Mr Pointless (the local delivery man) would lift them up, one on each shoulder and stagger up the hill with them to The Shop. Most times he would have them unloaded before Boyface had even woken up. Sometimes Boyface would hang out at the end of the pier, climbing on the piles of rusty, abandoned crates and look out to sea. On a calm day the pier felt like a runway, pointing out towards distant lands of adventure. When the sea was rough, the rickety old structure would rock from side to side like a boat and Boyface would pretend to be a ship's captain, navigating the waves.

'Who sends us the zebras?' asked Boyface.

'Ooh,' said Mr Antelope with a sucking sound. 'I couldn't possibly say. I'll tell you when you're older. But I think I'll have a wander down to the pier and have a chat with some people. See what I can find out about dodgy zebras.'

'Okay,' said Boyface.

'What are you going to do?'

'Well, I thought I'd run some tests on one of the Uncertain Ponies. See if there's anything wrong with it. Apart from the black and white stripes, of course.'

'Good thinking,' said Mr Antelope proudly. He was about to potter off but then his face changed and he looked at Boyface quite solemnly. 'You're very good at being a Stripemonger,' he said quietly. 'While

I'm gone, you are in charge.' Boyface gulped. 'Until I get back, of course.'

Boyface waved goodbye to his dad. Before he had time to think too much, the back door burst open and his friend Clootie Whanger marched into the kitchen with a pillowcase over her head.

'Are you poppinuponable?' shouted Clootie.

(Poppinuponable was a new word that Boyface and Clootie had made up. If you were poppinuponable it meant that people could pop in upon you for a chat and a piece of something nice. If you didn't want anyone to pop in upon you or you were green and puffy and ill, then you were unpoppinuponable.)

'I am poppinuponable indeed,' smiled Boyface. 'Sit down and have some horrible pancakes.'

Clootie Whanger did as she was told and Boyface took the heavy frying pan from the stove.

'Why are you wearing a pillowcase on

your head, Clootie?' asked Boyface.

'Well,' said Clootie, 'the saucepan was getting really boring.'

Since Boyface and Clootie's last adventure Clootie had taken to wearing a saucepan on her head. This was because she kept having juggling accidents and didn't want anyone to see the bruises on her face.

'I've found that the pillowcase is a lot lighter and doesn't clang around so much,' shouted Clootie. Clootie shouted most of the time and had one of the loudest voices ever fitted to a child. 'And I've cut eye-holes so I can see where I'm going.'

Boyface poured Clootie a plate of pancakes. 'You look a bit like a ghost,' he giggled. 'I think that's lovely.' Before Clootie had time to eat any breakfast, the Tartan Badger came thundering into the kitchen, jumped up onto Clootie's lap and gobbled up her pancake.

The Tartan Badger was officially the worst pet in the whole wild world.

'That's interesting,' said Boyface with a raise of his eyebrows. 'He doesn't normally eat pancakes. Hot food normally makes him sick.'

And just as he said that, the Tartan Badger made a disturbing snake-like movement with its back, emitted a nasty gravelly noise from its stomach and threw up all over Clootie's school uniform.

'Oh,' said Boyface. 'Sorry about that. I'll get you a dustpan and brush.'

'Never mind the dustpan and brush,' said Clootie. 'Get him off me before he does it again!'

Boyface picked up the creature, turned it on its back, and fiddled with its nose until it went completely still. Since his dad had shown him how to deactivate it, Boyface had learned a lot about the Tartan Badger and how to control it, which had meant the worst pet in the whole wild world changed the way it behaved. It was a lot easier to live with and had stopped biting his feet in the middle of the night.

Sometimes, it would even let him play with it. The creature would lie in front of Clootie and Boyface and stretch out on its back, showing off its tartan patterns and the three hand prints.

If you twisted its nose in the right way it would light up like a game and Boyface and Clootie would take it in turns to put their hands on the hand-shapes in the right order as they lit up in sequence. When they got it right, the Tartan Badger would do it again but faster and if they got it

right again it would go faster still. This would go on and on until the Tartan Badger could flash no further. Then the Tartan Badger would light up like a Christmas tree and do a little dance for joy whilst making a noise like a pair of farty spoons.

If they got it wrong it would try and bite their hands off.

'I do like the badger-light game,' said Clootie, 'but have you ever wondered why there are three hand prints?'

'Hmm,' said Boyface, stroking his chin. 'Maybe there should be three of us. Maybe we're supposed to meet another friend. Another friend who has the same birthday as us. I wonder what the Tartan Badger would do if all three of us pressed it at the same time?'

'Maybe we should spend today trying to find a new lovely friend.'

'Good plan,' said Boyface. 'But I've got to open The Shop and help Dad sort out these Uncertain Ponies.'

'Okay,' said Clootie. 'Maybe I'll find a third friend at school. There are lots of people there. I don't know if any of them have our birthday but I can ask.'

Suddenly, Boyface noticed that Clootie's voice had turned sad. He sensed that there was something she wasn't telling him.

'What's the matter?' asked Boyface.

'Well, I don't really like going to school any more.'

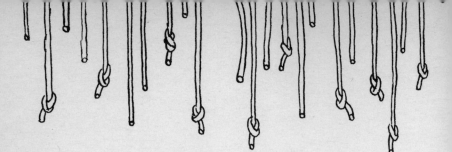

'Why not? What's the problem with school, Clootie?'

Clootie twisted her face and tried to explain. 'Imagine my head is a living room, full of furniture and toys and things to play with. There are soft, colourful rugs to lie on and loads of fascinating books, ornaments, trophies, and trinkets.'

'And this is the inside of your head?'

Clootie nodded and continued. 'In the corner, there's a television that's on all the time. I can't switch it off so I mostly ignore it. With school, it's like I'm being told that I should be watching the television because that's real life. I'm supposed to only watch this shouty screen in the corner of a room that has all this other fun stuff in it.'

'What happens if you watch it?'

'All the time I'm watching, I know there's much more interesting stuff going on behind me. I'm scared that one day I'll get sucked into the television and I'll forget about the important things.'

Boyface screwed his nose up and wiped some of the badger sick off Clootie's uniform with the back of his hand.

'What do you think?' asked Clootie sheepishly.

'I don't know,' shrugged Boyface. 'We've never had a television.'

'Fine,' said Clootie, in a bit of a huff.

'I'll just go to school then. Thanks for being so helpful. I'll call in on my way home and let you know if I've found a third friend.'

Boyface waved goodbye to his pillowcased friend and thought about doing the washing-up. Then he went into The Shop to fiddle with a dodgy zebra instead.

STRIPE THREE

Meanwhile, a small, oily boy called Oswald Muesli was riding his pony at the local riding school. His mother had bought the pony from Mr Antelope a few months before and had paid quite a lot of money for it – not knowing, of course, that it had started life as a zebra.

The riding school was at the top of the hill on the outskirts of the village, not far from the abandoned Ickle Chuff restaurant. Every weekend, the place was full of mostly reluctant children riding their ponies, or ones they rented from Marjory Indent, the poisonous woman who ran the school.

Marjory Indent was the meanest, thinnest-looking person you could ever imagine. She hadn't eaten a proper meal for nearly twenty years and survived on the tiny nutrition she got from the smell of horse manure and the comfort gained from the sobs of ungrateful children.

When Marjory Indent wasn't running the riding school she spent most of her time trying to organise her huge collection of scarves and co-ordinating them with her face. In her head she had a range of different faces such as:

 Beautiful

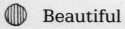 Mysterious

 Serious

 Joking

 Caring

 Understanding

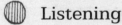 Listening

Marjory Indent thought that she should have a different scarf to match each face and spent many afternoons in shops looking for scarves of different colours and

patterns. In reality, of course, she only really had one face – a face of 'Anger and Meanness'. And to be honest, any scarf would have suited this face – preferably wrapped right over it so no one else would have to suffer the misery of looking at her.

On this morning, however, Marjory Indent was leaning over a fence, looking like a pair of scissors in jeans, watching Oswald Muesli and other boys and girls riding around the paddock. She was very cross indeed because half of her ponies had become Uncertain and turned into zebras. This made her really angry.

Worse than that, something even weirder was happening to the ponies – as Mr Antelope had predicted. They weren't just turning into zebras. They were also turning into all sorts of things. So far that morning, Marjory Indent had watched her prized school of expensive ponies change into sausages, Wendy houses, awkward-looking turtles, oddly shaped giant teapots, and an inflatable banana called Misty.

Clearly something very strange was going on. Marjory was furious.

'The problem is,' said a thin voice behind her, 'that the ponies have gone Uncertain. It's all happening on a quantum level.'

Marjory turned around to see a weird clown boy standing behind her. He was wearing the usual clothes of a clown. Bright colours, patches, massive shoes, orange wig, full clown make-up covering his whole face so you wouldn't recognise him even if he were your own child.

'And what would you know about ponies?' hissed Marjory.

'Probably more than most,' replied the clown. 'For starters, their heads are too big. It's not normal to have a head that huge and still be stupid.'

'Ponies are not stupid,' snipped Marjory.

'Yes they are,' insisted the weird clown boy. 'They never know what day it is and they can't do tricks or anything unless you choke them or whip them. If you hit me with a stick all day, I reckon I'd be happy to jump over anything you told me to and pretend I liked it. And why do you have to ride them anyway? Why can't you just leave them alone? You don't ride other animals. You don't look at a guinea pig and think – I know, I'm going to sit on that. You'd squash it.'

He was really ranting now and Marjory Indent was getting more and more annoyed with him.

'What really winds me up,' raved the weird clown boy, 'is when you put the pony in a trailer and tow it somewhere with a car. Surely the whole point of a pony is that it's a method of transport. You shouldn't be towing a pony. It should be towing you!'

Marjory Indent had had enough of his angry rambling. 'Stop talking!' she shouted at him. 'Just stop talking.'

He stopped talking.

'None of this,' screeched Marjory, 'explains why they are turning into zebras and ... other things.'

The weird clown boy smiled beneath his clown make-up, the colourful shapes on his face twisting and contorting. 'It's the Stripemongers,' he whispered. 'They have done this to you.'

Having got Marjory Indent's attention, the weird clown boy told her how the Stripemongers had been using The Machine to turn zebras into

ponies. He explained how they had sold her dodgy zebras and that something had gone wrong.

'What can I do about it?' demanded Marjory.

'Get revenge.'

'Revenge?'

'Yes.'

'How would I do that?'

'With this.'

As he said this he pulled something from one of his deep clown pockets.

'This?'

'This.'

The something was about the size of an orange. It was also the colour of an orange (which is orange) and had the same texture as an orange.

'It's an orange,' sneered Marjory Indent.

'No, it isn't,' grimaced the weird clown boy. 'It's a Quantum Disruption Bomb.'

Marjory looked at the orange.

'The Quantum Disruption Bomb,' he went on to explain, 'is a hand-held explosive device designed specifically to get revenge on the Stripemongers. It contains the one thing that the Quantum Chromatic Disruption Machine cannot process.'

'And what is that one thing?'

'Orange juice!'

The weird clown boy told Marjory Indent that all she needed to do was visit the Stripemongers' Shop and put the Quantum Disruption Bomb into The Machine. The Machine would then explode into millions of tiny pieces.

'And how will this help my riding school? Will it turn Misty the giant banana back into a pony?'

'Not exactly, no,' frowned the weird

clown boy. 'But it will ruin the Antelope family business and that should make you feel better.'

'Hang on a minute,' twitched Marjory suddenly. 'Do I know you from somewhere?'

The weird clown boy flinched like a cat. 'Of course not,' he gasped. 'I am just your friendly local villain. Happy to help you do nasty things in the name of awfulness.'

Marjory Indent had a quick think

about the situation, took the orange and marched down the hill, ready to cause some serious damage to the Quantum Chromatic Disruption Machine. Via her house of course – to find an appropriate scarf.

As soon as she was far enough away, the weird clown boy did something he'd been holding in for ages. He let out a massive sneeze and rubbed at his eyes.

Fibbernitchy (for that was his real name), was allergic to ponies. They

made his eyes itch and they made him sneeze and wheeze and probably would give him a sneezy wheezy disease of the knees. He was allergic to ponies, afraid of ponies, and he hated ponies.

'Big-headed pooflips!' he mumbled to himself. 'Hay-munching bumpackets.' He wandered back across the fields towards his Ickle Chuff hideout to carry on scheming against Boyface and his family.

When Fibbernitchy was born he was

perfect, just like a baby should be. But his mother wasn't happy with him. She wanted him to be different in some way. She wanted him to stand out, be fashionable, match some of her outfits. She tried dressing him in various expensive and exotic cardigans and baby-grows but it wasn't enough. She went to Mr Antelope's newly-opened Stripemongery. For the price of a fried egg sandwich and a packet of felt-tip pens, Mr Antelope put the baby through the Quantum Chromatic Disruption Machine and covered the baby in bright blue polka dots. The design was supposed to be temporary. It was supposed to only last for a few weeks. A month at most. But something went wrong with the quantum process. Somehow, Mr Antelope flummed it up like a proper poo flip. It might have been because he'd been having a bad day. It might have been that he'd made an honest mistake and forgotten to press the non-permanent candyflosserator. It might have been that he was very tired because he and his wife had just had their own baby boy and he hadn't slept for two weeks. Whatever the reason, the baby Fibbernitchy was left with permanent polka dots. They wouldn't wash off and would always be on the child's face.

His mother demanded that Mr Antelope reverse the process but Mr Antelope couldn't. She took the spotty Fibbernitchy baby to the doctor but the doctor told her there was nothing that could be done to help. 'The spots will come off as he gets older,' the doctor said. 'He'll grow out of it.'

But he didn't grow out of it. His mother took him to different doctors and each one would examine Fibbernitchy with a disgusted face. 'Eughh,' they would say. 'That's very nasty. But, there is nothing I can do.'

Friends and relatives would look at the baby like friends and relatives do, but they would screw up their faces with a gag and swallow a little bit of sick.

After a while, even his mother couldn't look at that polka-dotted face without putting a hand over her mouth and snipping, 'Ughh. How revolting.'

By the time Fibbernitchy was two he had accepted that everyone thought he was disgusting. And soon, he came to believe that he was disgusting.

By the age of three, he was more or less independent of his mother, having learned to cook, clean, use a telephone, and get money from the cash machine with his mother's bank card.

By the age of ten, he had created his own villainous hideout in the abandoned Ickle Chuff restaurant and was forming plans to get revenge on the Stripemongers and his chosen nemesis – Boyface.

He was particularly proud of the current plan to use Marjory Indent as a weapon to sabotage the Quantum Chromatic Disruption Machine. But it was only half of the plan. The other half was happening down at the pier and involved some dodgy fishermen, a trap, and a big boat that was scheduled to sail for a faraway land. It also involved some underwater sea donkeys that he had hired and a rusty old container that no one would miss if it was accidentally put on the next boat to Bahoumanoomaland.

'Nothing,' he thought to himself, 'can go wrong with this plan.' And he settled into his stainless steel lair for a cup of anti-histamine syrup and a cackle.

STRIPE FOUR

Back at The Shop, Boyface was working. He had a notebook in one hand and the other was darting backwards and forwards to his ear where he kept a tiny stub of a pencil. Whenever he used it, he would wet it first with the end of his tongue so that it wrote more smoothly.

The Shop was in a terrible mess. Even when it was tidy (straight after a spring clean) it was still the messiest shop you could imagine. Huge towers of nearly toppling piles of cardboard boxes had gathered together, struggling for a better view like cardboard-boxy meerkats. Bubble wrap covered most of the surfaces, and bits of machinery, large square batteries and rivets and brackets were scattered across the floor. Boyface had most of the Stripemongering manuals out and one of them was particularly useful.

It was called

LEARNING TO BE A STRIPEMONGER

Volume 9:
Problems With Stuff.

The Shop was particularly messy that day, however, because of the trouble with the zebras. There were piles of stripes lying all over the place and at least seven zebras were standing around looking uncomfortable. There was straw everywhere and the smell of the zebras was horrible.

Getting seven zebras into a shop is impressive but the biggest and most stunning thing in the room was, of course, The Machine. The Quantum Chromatic Disruption Machine had a curious ability to change itself while no one was looking. It was like it could eat bits of its own construction and then disrupt them into other bits which would stick out of holes and flaps where previously there had been something else or nothing. Sometimes it would seem to forget a thing or end up with an extra something left over. Occasionally,

Boyface would find a stripy screw or a spotty bolt lying on the floor and he could never work out where it might have come from. On this day, there were many bits and bobs sitting in a pool of oil right in front of The Machine. It was clearly struggling with all the zebras and the tests Boyface had been running on them all that morning.

Sometimes Boyface would plug the Tartan Badger into The Machine, download some Inklings and then take the Tartan Badger down to the beach where he would sit in the sunshine and use the worst pet in the whole wild world to change the colour of the pebbles – just for fun – or use it as a metal-detector. This day, though, wasn't really for having fun. He was trying to solve the problem of what on earth was going on with these Uncertain Ponies.

Boyface decided that the best thing to start with was an examination of one of the zebras, so he carefully stuffed one into The Machine's input bucket. The zebra wasn't really very happy about this but Boyface had become quite an expert at persuading creatures to go where he wanted them to.

Once the stripy fool was inside, Boyface activated the observation panel which slid back to reveal what looked like a cross between a dirty television screen and an inside-out fish tank. Once it had warmed up, Boyface could see what was going on at a quantum level.

(AUTHOR'S NOTE: A QUANTUM LEVEL IS THE LEVEL OF INCREDIBLY SMALL THINGS — THINGS SMALLER THAN YOU CAN SEE. EVEN SMALLER THAN A BEETLE'S NOSTRIL.)

To the human eye, the animal was a zebra. Viewed with The Quantum Chromatic Disruption Machine, however, it was many things all at once. Boyface could see the zebra but sometimes it was a grandfather clock. Then it would make a popping noise and turn into a bowl of custard. Then a pair of slippers, then a police car.

Something was very wrong with it. It was definitely Uncertain. Uncertain as to what on earth it was supposed to be.

Boyface thought it might be good to try disrupting the zebra to see if he could get it to stabilise as just one thing (preferably a pony) but he was interrupted by the tinkling of the bell above the front door.

Who was it? Was it his dad coming back?

No.

Was it Marjory Indent, coming to get revenge with Fibbernitchy's Quantum Disruption Bomb?

No. But she was indeed on her way.

So who was it?

It was Daddy-This and Daddy-That, two travelling salesmen who were passing through the area.

Daddy-This and Daddy-That were not their real names but they called themselves that so their son wouldn't get confused. Daddy-This was slightly taller than Daddy-That but couldn't jump as high. Daddy-That was better at numbers and counting and Daddy-This was better at words and talking. Between the two of them they were the best salesmen you could meet. They could have sold pogo-sticks to kangaroos if they'd tried. They were clothed in the dignified and impressive livery of a great brotherhood of experts, in patterns and stitches; notions and buttons; textiles and piping; bobbins and pincushions; pinking shears and elastic; eyelets and Velcro; seams and embroidery. Daddy-This and

Daddy-That were, you see, travelling haberdashers who wandered from town to town, village to village selling these things to anyone who would buy them, particularly shops who specialised in making things look different – just like The Antelope family's Stripemongering business.

'Ooh, hello, young man,' said Daddy-That enthusiastically. 'Is your dad here today?'

Boyface shook his head. 'He's gone to check on something at the pier. I'm kind of in charge while he's gone.

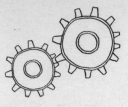

Can I help you?'

Boyface was worried that they
were there to complain about more
Uncertain Ponies but they were just
trying to sell patterns and fabrics.
Often Mr Antelope would buy rolls
of patterns from them to stick on to
things and creatures. He had once
improved a hamster by making it
paisley and the hamster had gone on
to win a competition.

Boyface wasn't authorised to buy
things without his dad and he

explained to the two men that it might be better to come back later when Mr Antelope was back from his mission.

'Very well,' sang the Haberdashers. 'We were thinking of looking around the village anyway. It seems like such a charming place to be.'

'There's a café over the road,' suggested Boyface. 'It specialises in cream teas and artichokes.'

'Scone With The Wind?' asked Daddy-This.

'That's the one. They do a lovely scone and the lady that runs the place might even read your fortune from it if you ask nicely. And pay her.'

'That sounds divine,' chirruped Daddy-That. 'Do you want to come too, Entelechy, or would you rather stay here?'

Boyface looked over his shoulder to where the two dads were looking. There was an almost invisible boy that he hadn't noticed at all. The boy said that he'd like to stay where he was so Daddy-This and Daddy-That left for the café.

Entelechy Venn – for that was his name – was a child with the peculiar skill of being almost invisible. It had evolved from the fact that he spent his days travelling the country with his two dads as their haberdashery assistant. Entelechy's role was to look after the samples of fabrics and patterns. He was a genius for making one thing suit another thing and he knew the names and tones of every possible colour you could think of.

Despite being ten years old, Entelechy worked pretty much full-time and

as a consequence he looked like his profession. His outfit, you see, was made up of many different samples of material, sewn together like a patchwork quilt. Silks and tweeds, wools and fleeces from head to toe, including a top hat and a pair of satin gloves.

Now, you might think that because of these clothes Entelechy Venn would only be truly camouflaged if you threw him into a pile of random curtains. But the boy must have been slightly magical because somehow he had combined his multi-patterned outfit with an amazing ability to stay perfectly still in various, impossible-looking gymnastic yoga poses. The combination of these things meant that Entelechy could stand next to some fancy wallpaper on his head and be unnoticed. Or he could lie on a complicated bedspread with his foot behind his ear and to the casual observer he would be almost invisible. Unless you were looking for him, you wouldn't know he was there.

On this occasion, Entelechy Venn

was sitting on the mouldy old sofa in the corner of The Shop with his legs crossed in the lotus position.

'I like your costume,' said Boyface. 'Your outfit is lovely.'

'And I like your machine,' said Entelechy crisply. 'What are you doing with all these stunning zebras?'

Boyface Antelope and Entelechy Venn became instant friends. Entelechy was genuinely impressed with all the patterns and stripes and polka dots and squiggles that were lying around

The Shop. He did have an urge to tidy it all up and put it in order, but he thought that would be rude. Instead, Entelechy kept his hands on the handle of the fabric samples case that he had with him and just concentrated on admiring the shiny curves and spell-binding pipes and nozzles of the Quantum Chromatic Disruption Machine.

Boyface explained to Entelechy what he was trying to do with the zebra and how it kept changing its shape and was turning into teapots, custard, and

police cars for no apparent reason. Entelechy was very excited by this.

'It's a bit like when you're getting ready to go out to a party and you can't decide what to wear,' he enthused. 'You start off with your yellow cords and they don't work so you start again with a pointy hat which you have no idea why you bought in the first place but it does go with a waistcoat that only works with the hat. Then you put some jeans on, first some light blue jeans and then some dark blue jeans and then you try a three-piece suit or some of those trousers with a fabulous sparkly stripe down the side.'

Boyface looked at his new friend. 'I have absolutely no idea what you are talking about,' he said with a smile. 'I just wear whatever is on the floor.'

Entelechy made an 'euuch' noise and did a sort of smile that made his mouth go rectangular. They agreed not to talk about dressing up for a while.

Boyface ran some more tests on the

zebra and Entelechy watched. The zebra was definitely unusual. It was certainly Uncertain and didn't seem to have any idea of what it was supposed to be.

While he worked, Boyface was wondering where his dad was. He had been gone for ages. He couldn't still be down at the pier, surely. Boyface wanted his dad to be helping with the zebra problem. Just as the word 'help' skipped through his mind, a strange reading came out of The Machine. It was on a ticket that

resembled a receipt that you might get from a shop. It came out of a slot near the top of The Machine, curled out like a duck's tail, and floated through the air into Boyface's hand.

#FFA500

'Oh no,' said Boyface. 'That's the code for orange.'

'Not orange,' whined Entelechy nervously. 'Nothing really goes with orange.'

'That might be true,' said Boyface.

'But it's more serious than that. Orange is the only colour that the Quantum Chromatic Disruption Machine can't cope with. It does terrible things to the insides. It could destroy The Machine completely. We never ever, EVER let anything that is pure orange into it.'

'Can it be any shade of orange?' asked Entelechy. 'Any old mixture of red and yellow?'

'No,' said Boyface quietly. 'It can cope with burnt orange or pale orange or lightning magnolia. It can even manage the sort of orange that you get on tigers. It's orange juice orange that sends it crazy. The colour orange that is the colour of an orange.'

'So what does that piece of paper mean?'

'It means that someone has contaminated the ponies we sold. It wasn't our fault. We put the zebras in The Machine. We took the stripes off them and turned them into ponies but someone has been feeding them orange juice. They have had an allergic reaction on a quantum level.'

Boyface picked up a volume of the Stripemongering manual, the one about problems and stuff. He knew it was the one he needed and urgently flicked through the pages until he found the answer he was looking for.

'Here it is,' he gasped. 'It's called Anachromatic Shock.'

'Well blend my borders!' said Entelechy. 'That sounds like what happens when you mix blue and green in an outfit. Could it really hurt that marvellous machine?'

'I shouldn't think these zebras would do any damage,' puffed Boyface. 'A little bit of orange in an Uncertain Pony is nothing we can't fix. It's only a disaster if someone were to put a whole orange into The Machine.'

Before Entelechy had time to respond, the door to the street opened and Marjory Indent strode inside. In her pocket she was holding a whole orange or – as she had learned to call it – a Quantum Disruption Bomb.

STRIPE FIVE

Marjory Indent was furious. Not just about the Uncertain Ponies but because all the way down the hill, someone called Adrian had got in her way. It had taken her twice as long to get to The Shop as it should have done.

She stood like half a spider, her skinny legs managing to make her skinny jeans look almost baggy they were so thin. Her pinched red face looked like it was being strangled by one of her many, many scarves (this one was pink with brown flowers on it).

'Are you a Stripemonger?' she growled at Boyface.

Boyface was terrified. There were bits of hay sticking out of her hair and he noticed that she smelled of manure. 'Is it about the ponies?' he squeaked.

'Yes it is,' screamed Marjory. 'You have ruined my riding school; ruined my business; and ruined my life.'

Boyface wasn't sure what the woman was going to do. 'I'm terribly sorry about that,' he said. 'My dad isn't here at the moment but maybe when he gets back ...'

'I'm not waiting for anyone!' shouted Marjory. 'I know what you've been doing. Fiddling with zebras on a quantum level and passing them off as ponies. And now I'm going to have my revenge. And I'm going to have it using this!'

She pulled the orange from her pocket and held it dangerously close to one of the Quantum Chromatic Disruption Machine's input buckets, high in the air with her crane-like arm. Boyface couldn't have reached it if he'd tried.

He was frozen stiff in panic. If Marjory Indent dropped that orange into The Machine while it was running, she could cause The Machine to implode and possibly create a mini black hole

which could suck the universe up
its own bottom. What was he going
to do?

'That's a very unusual scarf,'
Entelechy muttered, bringing his
suitcase into the middle of the room
and sitting neatly in front of it.
'It's a shame you don't know how
to wear it.'

Marjory was flabbergasted as she
hadn't even noticed the other boy.
'I beg your pardon?' she snipped.

'It's a most delightful pattern,' answered Entelechy, 'but the colours simply do not match your face, my dear lady.'

This intrigued Marjory. Matching scarves with her faces was, after all, very important to her. She took a step away from The Machine and two steps closer to the small boy. 'What do you mean?' she snorted, tossing her head back. 'This is my vengeful face and I chose this scarf because it matches the colour of my eyes when I am furious.'

'I'm sure you did, but it doesn't really work,' smiled Entelechy in a slightly mocking tone. 'Let me show you something that might interest you.' He opened up his case.

Boyface was still in a state of shock but was able to marvel at how Entelechy worked, distracting Marjory Indent with the smoothest of charm and the sharpest of knowledge about colours, patterns, and how to flatter a lady. Entelechy brought out piles of fabrics and scarves and draped them around

Marjory's scrawny neck, letting her feel the material against her skin and comparing their qualities with her sweater and bangles and overpriced wellies.

At one point he drew a diagram to show her what he was talking about. It consisted of two overlapping circles. One represented all the patterns in the world. The other represented all the different types of face she could have. 'The bit in the overlap,' Entelechy explained, 'represents the sorts of scarves that are right for your aristocratic bone structure.'

Marjory simply couldn't resist being complimented on her face or being pampered with co-ordinations and floral notions. She was the closest she would ever get to happy. Within minutes she had put the Quantum Disruption Bomb to one side.

Boyface quietly pulled the levers and pressed the buttons to shut The Machine down. With a final shudder and a bimbling peep, it was now safe from attack by orange juice.

While all this was going on, Mrs Antelope had come back from her property-stealing mission and had come into The Shop to check on her son. She put her head close to Boyface and watched the strange scene in the middle of The Shop floor.

'What's going on?' she whispered.

'Everything, Mum. Everything is going on.' Just having his mum close to him and feeling her breath on his ear made him feel safe again.

'Why is The Shop full of zebras?' she asked.

'They are Uncertain Ponies. People have sent them back because they went all weird. But I've worked out what's causing it.'

'Who's the boy in the funny outfit?'

'Entelechy Venn. He's a haberdasher or something. He's very clever with colours and he's helping that lady learn about fabric.'

'Why?'

'Well, that lady runs the riding school

and she was about to blow up The Machine with an orange bomb. He's distracting her.'

'So she's nasty?'

'Absolutely nasty. She's trying to ruin us.'

'Hang on a minute,' said Mrs Antelope and popped back into the house. She came back moments later with a bag of frozen peas. 'This should sort her out,' she said, walking towards Marjory Indent. 'Hey! Lady!'

Mrs Antelope yelled, swinging the peas over her head. 'Co-ordinate this,' and whacked Marjory in the face with the peas, knocking the poisonous woman out cold.

At that moment, Daddy-This, Daddy-That and Clootie Whanger came in through The Shop door. The travelling haberdashers had had a divine time having their scones read in the café. They were very excited because they'd been told that they would be staying in the village of Stoddenage-on-Sea for quite some time and should start looking for a home there.

Mrs Antelope picked up the unconscious Marjory and put her outside on the pavement like a bin bag. Entelechy popped a cushion under her head. The cushion was embroidered with a flowering of colours, perfectly complementing her face of surprised defeat.

Boyface explained to Clootie what was going on. He thought that all of the Uncertain Ponies could be put back to normal by using The Machine's juicing function to remove the orange juice atoms from their molecules. After that a daily dose of anti histamines and beige paint would keep them as ponies all the time. Certain ponies again. This would stop everyone complaining. Boyface wrote out a sign and put it on the front door of The Shop. It explained that anyone who had bought a pony from them should bring it back to a special Anachromatic Shock Surgery and he would extract the orange juice from them for no charge whatsoever.

Daddy-This and Daddy-That said that Entelechy could stay with the Antelopes for tea, so Entelechy, Boyface, and Clootie went up to Boyface's bedroom to play with the Tartan Badger.

'Did you find us a third friend at school?' Boyface asked Clootie.

'No,' shouted Clootie. 'They're all too boring. But it looks like you've made a new friend for us.'

Boyface and Clootie told their new friend their story and asked him when his birthday was. His tenth birthday had, of course, been on exactly the same day as theirs.

'It's like we are three matching clothes,' beamed Entelechy. 'A shirt, a waistcoat, and a snazzy bow-tie.'

Boyface didn't know what he was talking about, but Clootie was keen to show Entelechy the hand prints on the underside of the Tartan Badger. As Boyface caught it, turned it upside down, and deactivated the thing without it biting him, he remembered his dad. Mr Antelope had been gone all day now and hadn't come back. This was very unusual for Mr Antelope. He rarely went away and he always, always came back.

With this in mind, Boyface put his hand on one of the hand-shapes in the Tartan Badger's fur. Clootie did the same. Entelechy bit his bottom lip a little (he'd never really been sure about tartan) but nevertheless put his palm on the badger's belly.

CLICK
WHIRRR

As soon as the three hands were in place, the Tartan Badger started humming electrically. It twisted a little and curled up into a doughnut shape. The three friends didn't know what was going on. All they could do was watch as the creature's tail lifted up. And with a sound like the squeal of brakes on a bike, a bright blue light began to shine out of the Tartan Badger's bumhole.

'Bright blue light is shining out of its bumhole,' said Clootie.

'It's not bright blue,' whispered Entelechy. 'It's electric teal.'

Whatever colour it was, the Tartan Badger was doing an amazing thing. It was using the light as a kind of projector. The four walls of the room were turned into a three-dimensional cinema. The children looked around and realised that the light was projecting some kind of map. It could have been a map of the universe, or of the world. Or maybe a map of thoughts or connections. They weren't really sure. In the middle of his map there was a single flashing light. It was a strange thing to say but it looked like the light was in trouble of some kind.

'I wonder what that flashing light represents?' asked Clootie.

'Maybe it's us,' suggested Entelechy.

'Maybe it's Dad,' thought Boyface to himself.

STRIPE SIX

Stoddenage-on-Sea is a small place and as in most small places, word travelled fast. It didn't take long before everyone had heard about Boyface's sign and soon a long queue had formed outside The Shop. The queue consisted of half of the village holding onto zebras, sausages, Wendy-houses, trees, umbrellas,

awkward-looking turtles, a map of somewhere that hasn't been built yet, oddly shaped giant teapots, an inflatable banana called Misty, and a dog whose ears were so massive that every time it moved its head it boffed itself in the face. All of these things had once been ponies suffering from Anachromatic Shock. Boyface put the ponies through The Machine using the anti-juicing function, then fed them all anti histamines and a glug of beige paint. By tea-time, all of the things had been turned back into ponies and had been stabilised. Everyone was happy to have their beloved pets back and the problem of the Uncertain Ponies had been solved – for certain.

After some tea, Entelechy went away with his dads and Clootie went home. Both of them said they would be back in the morning. By bed-time, Mr Antelope still hadn't come back. Boyface went up on top of the roof. The underwater singing sea donkeys were out there in the waves, singing lullabies to each other but Boyface couldn't hear them. He didn't often sit up there by himself. His dad was

usually there for this bit. Just as he was about to burst into tears, the hatch opened. It was his mum. She wasn't used to the wobbly tiles on the roof but carefully strode over to sit down next to her son. She put an arm around him and pressed his face into one of her massive boobs.

'Ahmm mofffled burdard,' said Boyface, which is the sound you make when you say 'I'm worried about Dad,' whilst being muffled by a giant boob. 'He always comes home, doesn't he?'

Mrs Antelope looked like she was going to burst into tears herself. 'He does always come home,' she said as confidently as she could. 'He always comes home but maybe this time he's going to be a little late. I've asked down at the pier and no one knows what has happened to him, but something will come up. I've got a feeling that he might be gone for quite a long time.'

The two of them sat in silence for a while. 'What was the last thing your dad said to you before he left?' Mrs

Antelope asked. Boyface thought for a while.

'He said that while he was gone, I'm in charge.'

There was another silence. 'Do you think you can manage until he gets back?'

'Of course I can,' said Boyface with a new determination that he felt coming up from very deep inside him. 'I've got you. I've got the Tartan Badger, and I've got two wonderful friends. I can do anything.'

That night, in the abandoned Ickle Chuff, Fibbernitchy was pleased and annoyed at the same time. His orange juice plan had failed but his other idea was succeeding beautifully. Without his dad to guide him, Boyface would be much more vulnerable to attack. His vengeance on Boyface and the Stripemongers was progressing fairly well.

Back at The Shop, Boyface wasn't sure how he was doing. He felt like he was just putting one foot in front of the other and hoping that everything was going to be all right. Nevertheless, once he was settled in bed, he switched off his torch, went straight to sleep, and dreamed his day all over again.

THE END

Coming soon:

BOYFACE AND tHE
POWER of tHREE
AND A BIt